The Special Raccoon

*Helping a Child Learn
about Handicaps and Love*

written and illustrated
by Kim Carlisle

SMALL HORIZONS
An imprint of
New Horizon Press
Far Hills, NJ 07931

Dedicated to my daughters Glenna and Robin with Love.

Carlisle, Kim
The Special Raccoon: Helping a Child Learn about Handicaps and Love

ISBN 10: 0-88282-096-6
ISBN 13: 978-0-88282-096-5

SMALL HORIZONS
An Imprint of New Horizon Press

New Horizon Press books may be purchased in bulk quantities for educational, business, or sales promotional use. For information please write to New Horizon Press, Special Sales Department, PO Box 669, Far Hills, NJ 07931 or call 800-533-7978. e-mail: nhp@newhorizonpressbooks.com

Visit us on the web at: www.newhorizonpressbooks.com

2010   2009   2008   2007   2006   /   6   5   4   3   2

Printed in Hong Kong

One sunny, Saturday afternoon, Renna Raccoon and her new friend Bluebell Beaver were playing in the cool, shady woodland near Renna's den. The little girl raccoon and boy beaver were playing hide-and-go-seek among the green, feathery ferns. Bluebell was hiding quietly behind a large, fallen oak tree. Renna was searching for him everywhere.

"Bluebell, where are you?" Renna called, looking behind a big, gray rock. Bluebell scrunched his bushy, wide tail close around himself and didn't answer. He tried hard not to giggle. Renna searched only inches away from Bluebell's hiding place, but she still couldn't see him. Finally, Bluebell wasn't able to hold his giggles in any longer and a loud laugh burst from his lips.

Renna turned around with a jump. "There you are! I've found you!" Renna shouted with glee.

"Oh, you only found me because I laughed," Bluebell said as he skipped out from behind the log.

"Well, maybe . . . but I still found you," Renna replied.

"What do you want to do now?" asked Bluebell.

"Let's go to my den," Renna said. "I want you to meet my mom and little sister."

"Okay," Bluebell happily agreed.

As they walked in the woods toward Renna's home, she asked, "Did you know that my sister is handicapped?"

"No," answered Bluebell, looking uncomfortable. "What's wrong with her?"

"She's mentally and physically handicapped. She can't walk or talk. We have to help her do almost everything," Renna explained, watching her friend.

"Gee, that's too bad," Bluebell replied sadly. "I saw some handicapped people last week, but I've never talked to any of them before. What should I do when I meet her?"

"Just be yourself and be friendly," Renna said. She couldn't help worrying that her new friend would be afraid of her sister. She tried not to think of it. "Her name is Brookie, and she likes everyone. Look! There they are!" Renna turned away and hurried off toward her mother and sister.

Mrs. Raccoon was hanging some clothes out to dry in the warm, lemon–like, summer sunshine. Brookie was sitting beside her, waving a pretty yellow flower that she held in her paw.

"Hi, Mom! Hi, Brookie!" Renna said with a big smile. Then she bent down and gave her handicapped sister a big hug. She loved Brookie so much, no matter what.

"Hi, honey," said Mrs. Raccoon. "Is this your new friend?"

"Yes, Mom," Renna said, taking the little beaver's paw. "This is Bluebell. His family just moved into the pond at North Meadow."

"I'm glad to meet you, Bluebell," Mrs. Raccoon said, "and this is Renna's sister, Brookie."

"Hello, Mrs. Raccoon. Hello, Brookie," Bluebell said politely. He stared at the small raccoon who hadn't replied. "Can she hear me?" Bluebell whispered, looking back at Brookie a bit apprehensively. Bluebell's big, brown eyes widened.

"She can't speak, but she can hear you," said Mrs. Raccoon. "We're just not sure what she understands. She tells us things by pointing her paws or making sounds rather than using words."

Bluebell was very curious about this little raccoon who was looking at him with eyes as big and brown as his own. Bluebell knelt down closer to Brookie and said, "That's a pretty flower, Brookie. May I smell it?" Brookie just smiled. She didn't move. Bluebell put his paw over Brookie's and pulled the flower close to his nose. Bluebell took a deep sniff. "Mmmmmmmm, that smells good. Now you smell." Bluebell moved the flower near Brookie's nose and tickled her with it. Brookie started to giggle loudly. Bluebell said with a smile, "Maybe she can't speak, but she sure can laugh."

Mrs. Raccoon nodded. "Yes. She's a very happy little girl most of the time."

"Handicaps scare me sometimes," Bluebell said with a sigh. "When my mommy and I took some toys to the handicapped children at a hospital, I saw some little animals who couldn't walk or even sit straight."

"Some little animals' handicaps make them very upset," Mrs. Raccoon said. "I imagine it makes them angry not to be able to make their bodies do the kinds of things that you and I take for granted. You just need to remember that while they may look different on the outside, they're the same as you on the inside."

Just then, Brookie stuck the flower in front of Bluebell's nose again. Bluebell buried his nose in the blossom. "Look, she wants me to smell the flower," Bluebell laughed. He sniffed at the flower and sneezed. "Ahhhh Chooooo! Hay fever," he giggled. "Flowers make me sneeze, but I like to smell them anyway."

"I've finished hanging up the wash," said Mrs. Raccoon, picking up her laundry basket. "Let's go into the den for cookies and milk. Renna, please bring Brookie's cart over so we can wheel her inside."

Renna brought the wooden cart over to Brookie and lifted her up on it. "Since Brookie can't walk, this is what we use to get her from one place to another. My father made it especially for her," Renna said proudly.

"It looks like fun," Bluebell said, feeling more comfortable now. "Can I pull it?"

"Sure," answered Renna.

Bluebell picked up the rope with his mouth. He pulled Brookie toward the den. Brookie smiled and made happy sounds. She liked to ride on the special cart.

When they got inside the living room, Renna and Bluebell helped Brookie off the cart. They sat her on the floor, then placed a pillow beneath Brookie's body.

"The pillows will help support her while she's playing ball," Renna explained. The two new friends took turns rolling the ball to Brookie. As she tried to roll the ball back, it went in all directions. Renna and Bluebell laughed with glee as they chased it.

"It's more fun than hide-and-go-seek," said Bluebell. "How old is Brookie?" he asked.

"She's seven," answered Renna.

"Gosh, she's almost as old as we are," said Bluebell with surprise. Then he looked a little sad. "Will Brookie always be like this?"

"We don't know," said Mrs. Raccoon, speaking from the kitchen table. "She's able to do things better and better all the time. Sometimes, though, her progress can seem awfully slow."

Mrs. Raccoon looked up while peeling the tough green tusks from the corn cobs. "Bluebell, I believe that all of the animals with handicaps can think and feel just like we do. Their bodies and brains don't always work the way ours do; they can't always express themselves the same way we do. For instance, if you broke your arm and couldn't use it for a while, who you are wouldn't change . . . or when you get old and gray, perhaps you can't see or hear too well. No matter what, *you* are still *you* on the inside," Mrs. Raccoon said. "We can be thankful that doctors, nurses, therapists and teachers are always finding new ways to help *special* animals like Brookie."

"I understand," nodded Bluebell. "So even though Brookie can't walk or talk and do a lot of things that we can do, she's still the same as us on the inside."

"That's right," said Mrs. Raccoon. She picked up a plate and walked toward the children. "Now come and get your snacks. Renna, will you please feed your sister? I'd like to wash another load of laundry."

"Okay, mom," said Renna. She brought the plate of bugs and corn to where Brookie and Bluebell were sitting. "Here you are, Brookie. Doesn't this look good?"

Renna put a bug in each of Brookie's paws. Brookie ate the bugs one at a time. Then Renna gave her two more bugs. Brookie put both of the bugs in her mouth at once. "You like bugs, don't you Brookie?" Renna laughed.

"Do you want some corn?" Renna started scraping corn off a cob, so it would be easier for her sister to eat.

"How do you know she wants corn if she can't answer your questions?" Bluebell asked.

"Well, she'll either eat it or she won't," Renna explained. Renna poured a pawful of corn into Brookie's paw. Brookie grinned and shoved it into her mouth.

Bluebell laughed. "I guess she wanted it!"

"Do you want some water?" Renna asked Brookie, holding a cup up to help her take a drink. Brookie drank and drank until the water was gone. Then she rolled over onto her back as if to say that she was full.

"I'm full too," said Bluebell, rubbing his belly.

"Anybody home?" hollered Mr. Raccoon, walking through the front entrance and carrying a big, burlap bag.

"Hi, Dad!" said Renna excitedly. "What have you got?"

"I stopped by Mr. Rabbit's garden on my way home. I bought some carrots and celery," Mr. Raccoon said. He tossed his bag onto the table. "Would anybody like some?"

"No thanks, we're full. Mom just gave us a snack. Dad, this is my new friend, Bluebell."

"Well hello, Bluebell," said Mr. Raccoon with a smile. He came over to where they were sitting, hugged Renna, and then reached for his younger daughter. "How's my little Brookie?"

Mr. Raccoon swung Brookie up into his arms and gave her a squeeze. "Have you been staying out of trouble today?" he asked Brookie, ruffling the fur of the top of her head.

Renna giggled and said, "I don't know, Dad. This morning she took the top off the maple syrup and poured it onto the table. She got it all over her fur! She was so sticky and gooey! You should have seen her!"

Mr. Raccoon chuckled. "We can't turn our backs on you for a minute, can we little one? I guess you got a good washing in the stream."

"We had to wash everything Brookie touched, and she kept wanting to lick the syrup off everything. Mom was very upset!" Renna squealed. Then Renna started to singsong, *"Brook, Brook, Brookie full of gook, gook, gookie! She got so sticky, we had to wash her in the cricky."*

They all laughed some more.

"Well, Brookie, it sounds like you had quite a morning," said Mr. Raccoon shaking his head. "I guess that's why your mother has all of that extra laundry to do. It's a good thing we love you so much." Mr. Raccoon gave Brookie a pat on the head. Then he sat her back down on the floor. Brookie gave her dad a big wide smile. "Well, I'm going to Mr. Fox's market to get some eggs for dinner. I'll see everybody later. Nice to met you, Bluebell."

"Goodbye, Mr. Raccoon," said Bluebell with a wave.

"Wave bye–bye to Daddy," said Renna, helping Brookie wave her paw.

"Can Brookie dress herself?" asked Bluebell.

"No," said Renna, shaking her head sadly. "We do that for her, too. Sometimes it's a lot of work having a handicapped sister. But I love Brookie. I know she doesn't mean to mess up my homework or spill stuff."

"Yeah, I guess that would bother me too, but I think my brother is an even bigger pain and he doesn't have any handicaps at all," Bluebell replied with a sigh.

Renna nodded her head in agreement. "Sometimes it's hard to appreciate how others feel." She remembered how one of her classmates teased another little animal at the school playground last week and made him cry.

"Well, I guess I'd better go home now," said Bluebell, standing up and brushing corn kernels from his jeans. "My mother is probably wondering where I am."

Renna and Bluebell helped Brookie back onto her cart. Then they all went outside to look for Mrs. Raccoon. They found her down by the stream washing maple syrup out of the pretty red and blue checkered table cloth.

"Hi, Mom," Renna called, walking to the stream's rocky shore. "Can Brookie and I walk Bluebell halfway to the pond? He has to go home now."

"That sounds like a good idea," said Mrs. Raccoon. She leaned over to give Brookie a kiss on top of her head. "You'd like to go for a walk, wouldn't you pumpkin? I'll have to come over and meet the rest of your family some day soon, Bluebell."

"Oh, good!" answered Bluebell. "I'll tell my mom you'll be stopping by. Thank-you for the snack, Mrs. Raccoon. See you soon."

Mrs. Raccoon watched the three new friends go down the path. She felt very proud and happy that Renna and Bluebell helped care for and play with her special little one.

Strolling along the path, Renna and Bluebell took turns pulling Brookie on the cart. Sometimes they stopped to show her an interesting sight. They pointed out bright butterflies and blue birds, as well as a brown and white spotted deer dashing through the forest. They piled a whole heap of glittering rocks and differently colored flowers on her cart. Brookie smiled.

Renna and Bluebell felt good. They had helped Brookie see some new things.

When they got to the other side of the glen, they stopped to say goodbye to each other. "I'm so glad you moved into our neighborhood," Renna said to Bluebell.

"Me too," nodded Bluebell. He gave Renna a hug. "Now I not only have one new friend, I have two." He hugged Brookie tightly. Suddenly, Brookie reached up and put her little arms around Bluebell.

"She likes you," said Renna.

"Yes, and I like her too," said Bluebell happily. "It's late. I better get going."

"Wave bye-bye, Brookie," said Renna, helping her sister wave to their new friend as he started for home. Renna felt good because Bluebell liked Brookie. She knew that some of her friends felt uncomfortable around her sister, but Renna was glad that Bluebell had learned so much about handicaps and how very special each one of us really is.

—THE END—

Tips for Parents and Educators

1. Sibling interaction is extremely important because it is the first social network children experience and the foundation for their future social interactions.

2. Disabled or not, children first learn communication and social skills in the family setting and it is important to provide children with the right skills to deal with all types of social encounters.

3. All sibling relationships have their ups and downs, but the brother or sister of a disabled child has more emotional responses and concerns than a normal sibling.

4. Pay attention to the moods and reactions of the brother or sister of the disabled child and provide necessary emotional support and reassurances. Often they will have a range of emotions concerning their situation, such as guilt, ignorance about their sibling's condition, fear, embarrassment, anger, frustration, etc.

5. Don't forget that siblings have similar, if not the same, concerns as their parents regarding their disabled family member and they should be appropriately informed about their sibling's condition and be included in family concerns.

6. When siblings or other children ask questions about disabled children, parents and teachers should be age-appropriate, honest and direct.

7. It is important for parents and educators to teach siblings how to effectively communicate and deal with good and bad social situations they may encounter. Teach children how to talk about their brother, sister or friend's condition maturely, even in the face of teasing and mean remarks.

8. Do not pressure a sibling by giving them too much responsibility over their disabled brother or sister; remember they are children too.

9. Each sibling should be treated with equal emotional attention. Parents should take time to be alone with each child and encourage their individual growth.

10. Make sure non-disabled siblings have their own free time outside of their family situation and encourage them to effectively inform new friends of their brother or sister's condition.

11. Be aware of particularly stressful times for children and provide emotional support to minimize their burdens.

12. If a brother or sister is having an especially hard time dealing with their sibling's condition seek help from a professional support service that specifically deals with disabled child family situations.

13. Make sure that the non-disabled child is not trying to overcompensate for their sibling's disability by trying to be "perfect."

14. Inform children that being disabled is not a contagious disease and everyone is the same on the inside regardless of what someone can or can't do.

Tips For Kids

1. Having a disability is not a sickness and it is not contagious. People with disabilities are the same as you on the inside, but sometimes they can't do the same things you can.

2. Ask a parent or adult you trust to find out more about a loved one's disability so you can understand what they are going through.

3. It's perfectly normal to feel bad because you can do things that someone else might not be able to.

4. It is not your fault if you have a brother or sister who was born with a disability.

5. Don't try to be perfect or take on more than you can handle.

6. If you feel overwhelmed and frustrated don't feel guilty or hold it in. Tell your parents how you feel and why you feel that way.

7. Help out your brother or sister with things they might be struggling with and encourage them to do things that they can.

8. Sometimes people treat others unfairly because they are afraid of something new or different. Ask your parents or an adult you trust how to deal with unkind remarks.

9. Tell others when you think they're acting unkindly towards a disabled child and then tell an adult you trust.

10. Work with your family to come up with a plan to deal with difficult situations like someone staring, laughing or making fun of your brother or sister.

11. Get involved with activities at school and ask for time when you want to do something or just be by yourself.

12. Don't be afraid to invite friends over to your house because your brother or sister is disabled. Tell them about your sibling's situation and answer their possible questions truthfully.